WELCOM

PASSPORT TO READING

A beginning reader's ticket to a brand-new world!

Every book in this program is designed to build read-along and read-alone skills, level by level, through engaging and enriching stories. As the reader turns each page, he or she will become more confident with new vocabulary, sight words, and comprehension.

These PASSPORT TO READING levels will help you choose the perfect book for every reader.

READING TOGETHER
Read short words in simple sentence structures together to begin a reader's journey.

READING OUT LOUD
Encourage developing readers to sound out words in more complex stories with simple vocabulary.

READING INDEPENDENTLY
Newly independent readers gain confidence reading more complex sentences with higher word counts.

READY TO READ MORE
Readers prepare for chapter books with fewer illustrations and longer paragraphs.

This book features sight words from the educator-supported Dolch Sight Words List. This encourages the reader to recognize commonly used vocabulary words, increasing reading speed and fluency.

For more information, please visit passporttoreadingbooks.com.

Enjoy the journey!

Cover design by Jamie W. Yee.

Little, Brown and Company
Hachette Book Group
1290 Avenue of the Americas, New York, NY 10104
Visit us at lb-kids.com

First Edition: May 2017

Little, Brown and Company is a division of Hachette Book Group, Inc.
The Little, Brown name and logo are trademarks of Hachette Book Group, Inc.

The publisher is not responsible for websites (or their content) that are not owned by the publisher.

Library of Congress Control Number 2016948010

ISBNs: 978-0-316-31888-4 (paperback), 978-0-316-31887-7 (ebook),
978-0-316-55378-0 (ebook), 978-0-316-55379-7 (ebook)

PRINTED IN THE UNITED STATES OF AMERICA

CW

10 9 8 7 6 5 4 3 2 1

Passport to Reading titles are leveled by independent reviewers applying the standards developed by Irene Fountas and Gay Su Pinnell in *Matching Books to Readers: Using Leveled Books in Guided Reading*, Heinemann, 1999.

Licensed By:

TRANSFORMERS
ROBOTS IN DISGUISE

Decepticon Island!

Adapted by Steve Foxe
Based on the episodes
"Decepticon Island – Part 1" and
"Decepticon Island – Part 2"
written by Adam Beechen

LITTLE, BROWN AND COMPANY
New York   Boston

The Story So Far

Optimus Prime returns to help Bumblebee and the Autobots. They are also joined by an old friend who helps them learn more about the mysterious Decepticon Island....

The Autobots are chasing
a Decepticon when they run into
their old friend Ratchet.
Ratchet and his Mini-Con, Undertone,
help the bots capture the convict.

The Autobots' friendly reunion ends when an alarm sounds.

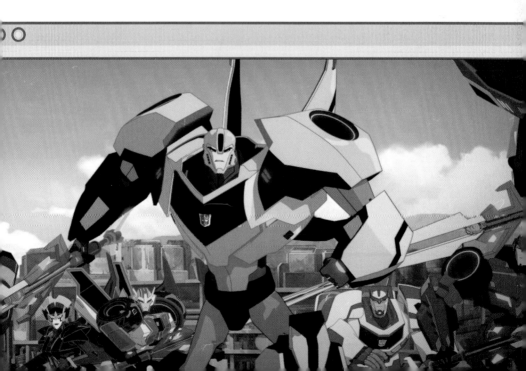

The bots find a Mini-Con.

He looks like Fixit,

but his name is Toolbox.

Fixit and Toolbox were together

on the prison ship the Alchemor.

Half the Alchemor crashed
into the ocean.
Now it is Decepticon Island.
Toolbox escaped from there.

Toolbox explains everything.

Steeljaw is in charge of

the Decepticons.

They plan to fix the ship, leave Earth,

and plunder the galaxy.

The bots need to stop
the villains.
Windblade has an idea.
They will use gas to knock out
the whole island.

Bumblebee has a sneaky plan
to reach the island.
Optimus thinks it is too risky.
They do it anyway.

The Autobots pretend to be
sleeping prisoners.
Grimlock disguises himself as
a Decepticon.
He drives a tugboat to the
hidden island.

The bad guys question Grimlock,
but they believe his story.

POW! BOOM!

Grimlock knocks out the guards.

The Autobots hurry into the crashed ship.

They sneak past lots of dangerous crooks.

The Autobots find some trapped Mini-Cons.
They want to help the Mini-Cons escape,
but the bad guys catch them.

Decepticons surround them.

"Welcome to my Decepticon empire!" Steeljaw says.

Windblade helps the others escape.
But she is captured.

While running, Bumblebee
drops his weapon!
Now Steeljaw has it!
This is very bad.

The Autobots split up.

Ratchet and Drift will rescue Windblade.

Strongarm, Sideswipe, and Grimlock
will release the Mini-Cons.

Bumblebee, Optimus, and Toolbox
will plant the gas bomb.

Fixit wants to help his friends.
He jumps into a boat and heads
to the island.

Ratchet, Drift, and their Mini-Cons
find Windblade and the Decepticons.
They fight the bad guys.

It is up to Jetstorm and Slipstream
to save their friend.
Once they free Windblade,
she takes down her jailer.

Grimlock, Strongarm, and Sideswipe fight
more Decepticons.

Groundpounder and Thunderhoof are tough,
but the Autobots are tougher.

Sideswipe uses a machine to knock out the bad guys and free all the Mini-Cons!

Bumblebee, Optimus, and Toolbox
find the main room.
Before they can set their gas bomb,
Steeljaw bursts in!

Steeljaw joins his weapons
to the weapon Bumblebee lost.
It gives him new armor and
makes him very powerful.

Bumblebee and Optimus fight
against Steeljaw.
Optimus lands a hit,
but Steeljaw shakes it off.
Bumblebee battles the Decepticon
but cannot hurt him.

Steeljaw thinks he has won.

That is, until he is shot with laser blasts.

"Mini-Cons, ATTACK!" Fixit shouts.

He leads his friends into battle.

Bumblebee arms the gas bomb.

The Autobots and the Mini-Cons
battle Steeljaw.
They get back the special weapon.

They change into their vehicle modes
and race off the island to safety.
They have defeated the Decepticons!

Windblade, Ratchet, and Optimus Prime
are going home.

The rest of the Autobots will stay on Earth.

"You are an excellent leader, Bumblebee,"
Optimus says.

"I leave this planet in good hands."